The Journey Overboard And Other Stories

Novid Shaid

DEDICATION

To our skipper on the sea without shore.

The
Journey
Overboard

Many miles underground, deep within the Earth's crust, there lived a subterranean race called the Porousees. They had lived underground, in their vast, intertwining tunnels, since the beginning of time, far from the sight of flora and fauna. What made them special was that they had the ability to talk like humans, sing like birds and carve patterns like artists.

Porousees were quite a sight to see. Their physique and features were much like humans, in fact, it would be accurate to compare them to the statues which the many human peoples sculptured of those they loved and revered. Consequently, Porousees walked on two legs; stood at good heights; with smooth, bare, solid bodies; made, some believed, from the rock of the marrow of the Earth. With finely-cut facial features and striking eyes, a swirling vortex of shining rock dust, a Porousee was both a handsome and imposing creature. They also had great strength and agility, and when they were manually hammering away in their tunnels, they covered the same distance and speed as the humans did with their drilling and grinding machines.

Porousees were genderless and, instead of reproducing the human way, some of them speculated that they grew from the Earth's core, perfectly formed, fully grown, brimming with vigour and vitality. Their births were traditionally known in the

Porousee language as "awakenings" in which from time to time, a newly-born Porousee suddenly appeared from the awakening tunnels. Typically, the new arrival climbed up these shoots, apertures dotted around the place, and emerged into this underground world, disorientated, confused. Then after receiving a name from his peers and living and breathing with his people, the new-born slowly gained speech, complex thought and great strength.

Strangely enough, the Porousees could not crawl back down these tunnels, which were just wide enough for an individual to crawl into. An invisible barrier would appear each time someone tried to climb in. Generations had attempted to pierce this magical property and crawl down it to see where it led, but they did so in vain, for they had never broken through in their history. This meant that, even in these modern times, the origin of the Porousees was an enduring enigma.

Porousees possessed the ability to think and speak which appeared miraculous for beings composed of solid rock. One could say that the Porousees were wholly magical creatures because their existence did not follow the logic of the humans who lived above them. Indeed, it only took a new-born a short space of time before he was conversing, and when he did, it seemed like he knew countless things. He could remember the great songs passed down through the ages, the myriad of names and terms for all the objects and ideas around them, even references to old beliefs and new beliefs about the world and where it supposedly came from.

Their existence totally contradicted all the studies that the humans had carried out about the possibility for the existence of creatures, dwelling near the molten, churning heat of the Earth's mantle. It was certainly hot in the Porousee tunnels, but being composed of pure rock, their bodies could withstand the pressure of the heat. Just the body heat of a Porousee would probably fry a human standing many metres away.

Another perplexing feature of this rock race was their acquisition of and adherence to the rules of human languages. They did not speak Neolithic groans and grunts, to the contrary, they articulated the language of the humans and even named themselves according to human words. Moreover, this species led almost parallel lives to the world way above. Many Porousees who believed in the old ways held humans in high esteem, believing their fate and abilities were inextricably linked. What's more, they were never supposed to meet with the humans or mix in their world, though they knew a great deal about the human realm, and in their songs and stories, the Porousees passed down a whole canon of tales which depicted the lives of mankind.

Traditional Porousee lifestyle involved digging and maintaining the magnificent networks of tunnels that they lived in. Some tunnels stretched way into the distance, and a Porousee could walk for the human equivalent of days and days and not see a tunnel come to an end. If you can picture a rabbit warren, except deep enough so that each tunnel could reach way up, hundreds of metres, and grow wide enough for thousands of furry rabbits to fit in, you can begin to picture a typical set of tunnels in the world of the Porousees. The tunnels, endless and interlocking, represented innumerable years of work and dedication by the many generations of Porousee people. There were now so many tunnels and Porousees that there was almost a population big enough for a fair-sized human country living there by the Earth's mantle.

Being underground could be exceedingly dark, but the Porousees had overcome this problem. It's true that the first generation lived in a primeval gloom and had performed an amazing feat of digging and carving in the darkness, until after a few generations, they finally uncovered the luminous rock which lit up their world.

The Porousees would sing eulogies praising the first generations, speculating that they had amazing abilities and possessed eyes which illuminated the world around them, but as time went by, this luminescent quality appeared much weaker in the following generations.

As the early generations had dug so high, lighter, luminous rock, which the humans called "radioactive", beamed down light, powerful enough for these beings to move around and see their world effortlessly. This light was very much like the twilight that humans were used to as the sun is setting, only the Porousees lived in this light every day, and time seemed to merge together into one relentlessly shifting mass. Porousees measured time according to their sleep and measured distance according to the number of tunnels they walked past. Phrases like: "Fifty tunnels ahead" or "A few sleeps before" or it will be done "Within a sleep" were familiar to their vernacular.

Without a doubt, an awe-inspiring sight in the tunnels was the glorious wall carvings and patterns which Porousees had created and etched. For these creatures spent their time engaging in three complementary pass-times: digging and deepening the tunnels; telling each over stories; competing in verse and also etching an infinity of rock patterns and creations, symbolically representing their existence.

Porousees did not draw themselves or any faces, rather they drew symbols, and depicted the myriad of rocks and shapes around them, producing some highly intricate patterns which covered miles and miles of the tunnel walls. Having strong, artistic and skilful hands, these rock people could manipulate segments of rock and turn them into versatile tools used for breaking through and smoothing down solid rock. They had knives, splints, shovels, hammers and elongated, nail-like maces which they used to dig into the walls and etch their patterns.

So, they spent much of their days working in their tunnels, churning away rock face, after rock face, without ever coming near the open air of the humans. The rest of the time, when they were not digging or patterning, the Porousees relaxed, gathered together in circles and told each other stories of their past, of the humans above, and they recited timeless songs which contemplated their origins and praised their world. It seemed as if these people were born to speak and sing and represent their world through symbol, patterns and song. This was their reality, because apart from working and decorating the tunnel walls, sleeping or training the new-borns, they did not have much else to do. They did not require sustenance because they were composed of solid rock and the Porousees did not feel human emotions like romantic love, although they understood and felt the love of their comrades and their own race. Some could even become highly strung during the debates about the origin of their existence and the nature of things.

The Porousees had a great fraternal instinct which meant they lived in unison and cooperation. No individual had ever governed or led them, like an Indian chief for example, instead they decided on things with an instinctive sense of brotherhood and consultation. They had heard of the great human leaders like Caesar, Alexander, Genghis Khan and their like, but none ever yearned to promote himself above the rest, although times were beginning to change in this regard.

Certainly, up until now, instead of relying on days or nights to rule their time, they all slept at the same time, in almost like a domino effect and, similarly, they all awoke in symphony. And they all slept together, in circles dotted around the place, on the ground, unlike the humans snoring away in their quilt and mattress beds. Food they did not require, but sleep, they did. Many even had dreams like humans.

So, after a hard day's work in the tunnels, a typical sight was hundreds and hundreds of groups of Porousees, huddled in circles, talking away, the words flowing like waterfalls from their mouths. But then, one by one, suddenly, they would gently fall to the ground and sleep, soundlessly.

However, one inexplicable reality had always haunted the lives of these rock people, which they had never been able to fully explain, which was more baffling than their births: "The Journey Overboard".

These days, many Porousees insisted on calling it simply, "the disappearance". Whichever idea they chose to believe, this phenomenon involved a sad and mystifying event. At any given time, any one of the Porousees would suddenly become entranced and silent, leave his friends and walk far away into the tunnels. So far and so long that he would never be seen again. It was as if their consciousness was wrenched out and all that was left was an empty shell that just walked and walked until eventually it disappeared without a trace.

And once again, without explanation, the other Porousees could not save those who came under such a spell. Something like an invisible force-field prevented the others from touching or following the disappearing Porousees, who would move away at an amazing pace, unstoppably. Porousees were strong, but there was an ebb to their energy which naturally impelled them to rest and sleep and once they awakened their energy would return. So, however painful and troubling it was for those left behind, they all knew at the back of their minds that they would one day go through the same event and many feared that day. Consequently, over the years, many stories emerged and circulated about what occurred after a Porousee "disappeared".

There were a collection of myths and beliefs about the birthing tunnels and the disappearances, but the most enduring of them all, which had lasted the test of time, was traditionally called "The Journey Overboard". This was related to an ancient and bizarre belief that most of the Porousees were beginning to reject in these modern times.

The belief was that their origin was not of the Earth's core. Their origin was from a vast endless entity, "the sea", which was composed of a mythical property called "water", which humans depended on, a transparent and formless liquid which was supposed to flow through every living thing. Indeed, their very name, Porousee, was derived from the word, "porous" which meant absorbing water, and this illustrated how prevalent this belief was with the early generations.

The myth went on to explain that they did not live underground, but on a vessel called "a ship" which was so vast that it could house the whole world of the Porousees and the humans, but there was a subtle trick involved in this which very few could explain. The ship floated on the infinite sea, under the sublime sky, warmed by the benevolent sun. These two heavenly spirits gazed down upon the sea and were but manifestations of the ocean's warmth and vastness.

So, when a Porousee lost his consciousness, he did not disappear. Instead he was pulled back to his original home: the endless sea without a shore. When a Porousee went on that journey, after many days of silently advancing through the tunnels, he would encounter a trapdoor in the wall above, and through the trapdoor he entered onto the deck of the ship and then jumped overboard, with all the humans, into the sea without a shore, from whence he came.

None could explain all the details; this was just what those believed in the past. They could not explain how you reached the sea once on the deck, especially if this ship was so vast, that it must take ages to reach the end of it. Many others questioned this element, water, which they had never seen or felt in their subterranean abode but had heard about in the human stories; how could they believe they originated from something they had never seen or felt?

This was why in these modern times, most now chose to believe that they lived on a place called the Earth, with the humans perhaps living way above, but then many were even questioning the existence of humans, and some were even doubting whether they existed near the Earth's core.

In recent times, there was a large group of people who rejected the name Porousee and were labelling themselves something rather provocative: Imperveites.

These Imperveites ridiculed and mocked those friends who still held onto that idea about the ship and the sea, which they said was ignorance that their elders followed. They chose to believe in what was closer to hand and easier to prove. Many of these ones were questioning everything about Porousee culture and lifestyle. Was there any actual benefit in continuing their digging and endless swirling patterns? There was enough space for the Porousee population. Why didn't they manipulate their tools to build on the ground they lived on instead of blindly digging on like their elders did? Others thought they should dig upwards and live with the humans. Some thought they should concentrate on following the disappearing ones and piercing the shoots so that they could find the truth behind their emergence and disappearance once and for all. The fraternal spirit of the Porousees had somehow been shaken and tossed aside.

Just as the humans above were reaching a point of despair and frustration, the Porousees were following suit, displaying behaviour and emotions they had, hitherto, never shown. One could say there was even a hint of pride and hatred creeping into the Imperveites who stubbornly suggested that all should follow their way.

**

These days, Darya felt turmoil, an emotion he had never felt before. He was one of the few Porousees left who still believed in the old myth about the ship and the sea, while his erstwhile friends had all transformed into hard-nosed sceptics, renaming themselves Imperveites, sneering at anyone using the old names.

They had proudly chosen new names for themselves. The old names were all related to water, the sea, the mythical ship and the waves which were like swelling and rising shapes in the sea. Interestingly, all the Porousee names were derived from human words and the old Porousees held humans in a high regard, considering them as almost superior creatures because they lived closer to the sea on the deck.

But now the Imperveites chose to name themselves after the rocks around them. Why call yourself by these stupid old names related to some mumbo jumbo? Names like Bahr, Marina, Callan, Maris, Jeevika were replaced with Sediment, Granite, Ironite, Coalite and others. The Imperveites insisted that their names should reflect the world around them and not some alien idea which those before had not questioned nor proved.

Darya's friends attempted to persuade him to join them and after a long debate, which was beginning to turn ugly, his friends left him, marching down the caverns, joining the growing masses of Imperveites. Indeed, two groups were now neatly forming themselves. The growing majority was the Imperveites, who gathered together in vast concentric circles and stood, like sentries, outside the birthing tunnels, ready to educate any new arrivals. They had chosen their leader, one of the previously best-known carvers and speakers, formerly Adrie, now Vaste, who had suddenly rejected his crafts and decided all their work was in vain. He violently hated the patterns now, so much so that he wanted to destroy all of them, which was near enough impossible.

In horror, another emotion Darya had never felt before, which made him sick to his very core, he watched as the groups grew apart gradually, until only a humble group of Porousees remained in clusters, on the outskirts of the tunnels, while the Imperveites dominated the scene, and now seemed to be calling the shots.

"My fellow friends!" proclaimed Vaste, giving his promotional speech to a vast gathering of newly converted Imperveites and some new-borns in the middle of his tunnel. "I see no reason that we should waste any more time. The time has come for us to make a choice. A historic choice. A choice which no other friend in our history has ever dared to take. A choice that involves transforming our future. We are all agreed that those of the past have had their time, and their legacy is these meaningless tunnels and carvings and diggings that we have imitated without questioning why.

But no more my friends! No more of this stupidity. Now we will choose between two things.

Either we become just disillusioned nitwits blabbering on about the stupidity of the past or we choose to build on what we have, build structures like the humans and we could live in a more industrious way, where we have better rules and processes. We have to find a way of enhancing our circumstances, of progressing more than any of us have dared to do in the past.

We have to accept that we will never discover our fate. We were never meant to, one day we are all going to walk away and that's it. And more and more of us will just continue to be born and take over from where the others left off.

We must progress. We must move forwards.

So, I say, that we first start by building ourselves structures and roofs so that we can live in a more dignified way, instead of sleeping on the ground, like an extra layer of dust. We should believe in our own worth. All new-borns should now be taught according to the new way. And though we will miss any of us who has disappeared, we will no longer dwell on where they have gone to. It is none of our concern anymore. Our only concern is the here-and-now and the future of our people."

Now Vaste took a step forward impressively: "We should also choose who will lead us. The humans had their Alexanders and Caesars. Those who were brave enough to step into the future.

So, our new future will start from there. And I am the one who is brave enough to take us forward. What say you?"

The Imperveites looked at each other, as Vaste towered above them, staring coldly and superbly around him. They were all impressed by his oratory skills; they were almost spellbound, for no one had ever promoted himself before like Vaste. This was something new. Previously, the Porousees simply debated and sang differing songs, giving each person a chance to speak. They never needed leaders before. But the Imperveites were changing things rapidly. It felt like Vaste had something special, which nobody else had displayed before. So, they all raised their hands in submission and shouted:

"We are with you, dear Vaste! We are with you!"

Vaste suddenly shuddered in delight. Before, when he recited the tales and poems, the applause and appreciation were less gratifying than this. Before, the people thanked him for summoning the spirits and tales of the past and the humans above, but he wasn't the focus, rather the tales were. Now all eyes were on him, with almost a feeling of worship and grandeur and this feeling sent surges of elation into every pore of Vaste's impressive frame.

"Thank you, my dear friends! Let me remind you that we still have yet to convince the others of our plans and I urge you to bring them with us and discard the ways of the past."

"But dear Vaste! We have tried," shouted one of the crowd, "And they stubbornly hold on to their ways, they insist on carving and telling the stories of ignorance! They will not listen."

"Well, then you must give them some more persuasion of the harder sort. We must have all our friends working together towards one common goal; we can not have any weak rocks in our walls, otherwise the wall will eventually crumble and collapse. We must deal with the ignorant ones..."

Darya listened from behind a large rock with fear and anxiety; more emotions sickening his heart. These were terrible times, in which his whole world seemed to be fermenting and convulsing around him. He did not know what to do. When his friends had striven to convince him, he just could not accept what they had to say. For he believed in the sea and water. He loved it with his whole being and always had. He spent hours carving his own images of the sea which he depicted as rising and falling lines, conjoined and symmetrical, sometimes rising way high up the rock walls and sometimes calmly levelling off. He even dreamed of the sea. He heard it... A whispering, infinitely echoing soft voice which rose and fell like a wondrous spirit.

So, when they came for him, he refused to accept the new Imperveites and their ways. And when he challenged them, he saw an expression that he had pictured when hearing the stories about human-beings: hatred. They narrowed their eyes, and glared at him as if he was a fool. He did not know what they would do next. In the stories, the Porousees had heard of the humans and their conflicts, which Porousees understood were specific to the human condition and not theirs. But now Darya could see that they themselves were displaying qualities of the humans.

"Hey! Watch where you're going friend!"

Darya stumbled into someone as he edged away from the rock.

"Oh, I apologise friend, I didn't see you there. Do I know you?"

Darya stared at this individual and could not recognise him.

"Oh, I am not from these tunnels," replied the stranger, rather short, with a constant smile on his face. Darya knew this one was still a Porousee.

"I was just walking through, looking to see if your tunnels were following the new way."

He looked ahead and heard the cheers and gazes directed at Vaste while he spoke a distance away.

"To my dismay, it seems that most of you have as well. I have never felt dismay before. Thought only the humans felt it. But then so much is not as it was before." He looked to the distance, regretfully.

"I don't understand what is happening to us. I thought that we could never change like this. I thought it was in our nature to dig, carve and sing and that was it. We don't fight like the humans. I thought things couldn't change." Darya was hoping that this stranger could somehow provide some answers.

"Well, things are changing; we can see that for sure. I don't know what to do myself, but I think there is someone who does. His name is Bahrun, the legendary skipper on the sea without a shore, and I have heard that he is one of the oldest Porousees left. He's been through more sleeps than the number of rocks on the floor."

And now the stranger reached forward to whisper in Darya's ear, "Some say that he has even travelled through the tunnels and found the trapdoor and seen what is there with his own eyes..."

"Why have I never heard of this one?" Darya was beginning to feel a little sceptical of this little Porousee but the hope was overpowering.

"Why, have you travelled through all the tunnels? Do you know all the friends who live, dig and sing? There are hundreds of us, if not thousands. I have walked and slept many times before I have got to you and I have seen the same thing. All our friends dropping their tools and coming here and following the new way. So, I thought I would follow them and now that I can see where they are going, I have decided to find this fellow, Bahrun, the skipper. Do you want to join me?"

A roar of laughter and applause shook the ground as Vaste was telling a new tale about the future and stupidity of the old ways.

"Well, I will probably be the only Porousee left here and I am afraid what these new ones will do. I used to call them friends and we used to carve the walls together but now they are not my friends, though I wish the best for them. I will join you."

"Excellent, by the way, my name is Mesi."

"And I am Darya."

This brought a smile to Mesi's face. "Let us make haste, before these friends of the future take note."

"Hey you two!"

Darya and the Mesi were just about to walk away, but turned to find a group of Imperveites hailing them.

"Come here now; we want to talk to you."

"Do not answer them. Let us pretend we never heard them and move ahead to the next tunnel." Darya followed Mesi's instructions and moved towards the entrance of the tunnel, which opened into four new tunnels leading in different directions.

"Hey, we're talking to you!"

Darya heard thumping steps running towards him.

"Oh great!" whispered Mesi. "They've found us."

"Now what?" Darya looked behind him to see a dozen Imperveites rushing towards them, more like guards than his erstwhile friends.

"How rude of you!" A dozen reviling faces surrounded Darya and Mesi.

"Look we are so sorry. We were just sitting here and decided to leave. We didn't hear you."

Another roar of laughter shook the ground from Vaste's epic speech.

"As you can hear, your meeting must be very enjoyable, which is why they are cheering and we didn't hear you calling to us." A hint of sarcasm was entering Mesi's voice.

One of them stepped forward.

"Darya?"

Darya looked and found his old friend Callan, now Ironite, glaring at him with not a single trace of their friendship left. Darya's heart dropped and he looked to the ground.

"What are you doing here? You love your carving and the old stupid ways. Have you changed your mind? I don't think so. For we tried to convince you and you just revealed how ignorant you are. Perhaps you were spying on us?"

"Spying?"

"Yes, you know what the humans do. When they listen to other humans secretly then go away and tell their friends, so that they can plot and plan. What a shame it is to see our kind acting like the ignorant humans." Darya could sense a frightening bitterness in Callan's voice.

"Look, we are just leaving. We are sorry for disturbing your meeting. Farewell Callan." Darya paused and realised his mistake.

Callan moved in closer to Darya: "My name is Ironite. Dare you name me like that again and you will be sorry. You should change your name from Darya to Dust, for you are worth nothing more than the dirt that lives under our feet. Let us leave these simpletons to themselves." And Callan and his group moved off back to the speech.

Mesi looked up at Darya sympathetically while Darya looked down at the ground, shifting the rock dust between his feet.

***

Time moved on. The nasty meeting with Callan and his foot soldiers faded into the distance, but left a lasting effect like a stubborn odour in the air. Darya struggled to understand how Callan could forget their friendship so easily. Callan, who he had sat with and laughed at the same stories, whistled the same tunes.

So, they walked through many sleeps and tunnels in what seemed like ages. In each tunnel they noticed similar personalities like Vaste taking centre stage, dazzling their followers, embracing the new, rejecting the old. They noticed small groups of Porousees way up in the walls, continuing to carve and dig, but hesitating and looking behind them in case they were being watched. Once they saw a group of Imperveites wrestle some carvers away from their work and steal their tools so that no more work could be done. As time passed on, the Imperveites seemed to be developing more and more aggression and intolerance, which Darya and Mesi could not help but find disconcerting.

However, despite the worries, Darya was both bewildered and exhilarated by his present excursion with his new-found friend, Mesi. The sight of Porousees shaking their fists and reviling the old ways was disheartening, but the new faces, the unique pattern formations on the walls were exquisite to behold.

Each set of tunnels presented its own swirling matrices and geometries. Innumerable images and depictions all represented a shared vision which had held the Porousees together as a whole entity, but now, sadly, the rebels seemed to be resisting and convulsing, as if they were disentangling themselves from the threads of the past, severing ancient ties.

"Here we are!"

Darya looked ahead to see a great hall of a tunnel, wide and rocky, with a circular gathering of Porousees seated, lost in the throes of an old song they were chanting together in one voice. Their eyes were closed and they seemed to be completely unaware of their surroundings. These people had certainly not changed from the old ways and Darya noticed that through their behaviour and demeanour, most of the groups were more advanced in their ages. Porousees did not age physically, for their smooth bodies withstood the test of time, but the eyes and the voices revealed it. There was a quality in their voices and a deepness in the eyes which revealed greater experience and depth. As he listened, Darya was intrigued because he understood the basic elements of their song, although he had never heard the lyrics or melody before:

Gaze with your heart, you'll see
A never-ending sea
Its water is the wine of Unity.
To set this secret free,
You need to turn a key
Unlock your door gaze at Eternity.

The circle of Porousees recited this piece of verse, swaying and rocking to and fro, like Darya's patterns of the mythical sea etched out on the cave walls. The group seemed to slowly rise together as one body and then fall weightlessly as they intoned their song:

Plunge headfirst in the Sea,
Keep diving endlessly,
Drown in the waves of this pure entity.

Their hypnotic chanting came to end and they returned to themselves, gazing around slowly, then moving off in various directions, some in Darya's direction.

Suddenly, an almighty force seemed to flow straight into Darya, engulfing him for moment, surrounding him in a whispering surge, a whisper that he had heard somewhere before, in what seemed like a hidden, forgotten thought in the recesses of his mind. Darya winced as this invisible presence rushed through him, until he came to his senses, somewhat bewildered and before him and Mesi, stood a Porousee of the most singular quality.

He looked timeless. His eyes swelled and plummeted forever and when he spoke, his soothing vibrating voice resounded, as if his voice echoed back and forth from a bottomless chasm. Darya was struck for words.

"Welcome dear friends to our humble abode. What brings you here?" smiled the old Porousee.

Mesi looked at Darya first, but found him muted with awe so he carried on.

"We have come to seek out the one who is named Bahrun, the skipper, for we heard he is old and wise and can give good counsel in these changing times."

"Oh, I see. You are both looking for some answers," and he gazed calmly at Darya, who now seemed to be finding his feet again after his abstracted moment.

"Our world is changing," declared Darya. "For hundreds and hundreds of sleeps, all we have done is sing the great songs of past, carve the walls with our beautiful lines, tell stories to each other of what might be and sleep without a care in our hearts. But now our people are not that way anymore. For the first time that I can remember, I don't know what to do."

The old Porousee smiled and said: "Do we always need to know what to do?"

Darya thought for a while, slowly becoming irritated.

"Of course, we do. For how would we move forward and find a way to help ourselves if we did not know what to do."

The old Porousee looked carefully at Darya, as if gazing into his heart. "The answers to your question do not lie in moving forwards, the answer for you lie in moving upwards."

"Upwards?"

"Yes, upwards, where the sea without a shore rocks and sways, where our ship floats and rushes along the sea, moving onwards but never going anywhere, because the ship is not important, once one has recognised the sea."

Darya had been listening carefully, while Mesi was wrapped and stunned by this venerable man.

"I take it that you must be Bahrun, and you still believe in the sea."

"Indeed, I am and I knew I would meet you some day, when our people were beginning to do things they had never done before, when the humans were suffering under the hands of cruel friends and were losing their way. It is the time near the end, when the ship begins to lose its float, when the ship begins to sink in the depths of the sea, and all of us whether we like it or not, plummet into the depths of the sea, either sea birds, flying into the waves, or useless rocks stuck onto the seaweed on the sea floor."

"I don't know what to say?" Darya had certainly been moved by Bahrun's revelation, but the fear was still fresh inside him.

"How can you be sure of what you say? And what does it have to do with me? All I desire is for life to return to way it once was. My desires are simple, just as all our people have always had, to dig deeper into the Earth so that our people can thrive, and carve our world so that our people can live in wonder and beauty. Where can I find this again?"

Bahrun moved forward to Darya and took him by the hand:

"Let me tell you, my young friend. I recognise you, though you do not know me. What you are looking for, I am afraid to say, will never return. The new way has arrived, it is as clear as the light off our walls and as strong as the rock that we sit on. Many will discard the old and take on the new. But there will always be those who know their origin, who know what lies deep within..."

"What is this origin?" Darya was now caught in the old man's gaze.

"Water. Pure unadulterated water. Water, so clear that you can see the whole world through it, and so free, that it rushes forward in one body, enveloping all with its powerful embrace. Water can flow through us, though we are not composed of water ourselves, but we feel it because we are the Porousees. We may be hard rock and our bodies may be able to burn the whole of the human world and all its life, but we are porous, we were fashioned by the sea, as were the humans. I learned from the sea without a shore that every living thing originates from water. Everything has its origin in this clarity. So, without the forever-rolling sea, we would not be here today. And now, the sea is calling us back, but as you know, most are in a state of denial."

"I have heard the sea in my dreams."

"And many have even beheld it with their very eyes..."

Mesi stirred: "And you, O Bahrun, our skipper, please tell us about the stories that are told about you in the tunnels from which I came. They say you found the door and went to the world above where the sea encompasses everything. They say you are one of the skippers of the great ship on the sea without a shore. Tell us what you saw."

Bahrun smiled. "There is a piece of verse that I love to sing which I hope I will sing before the sea calls me back:

Once I saw its waves, rising beyond
And since then every speck of dust
Reminds me of the sea without a shore
How I long to see its water clear as day
Reflecting the blazing sun and the magnificent sky
My body may be solid impenetrable
But water flows through every pore."

Bahrun closed his eyes and gave an almighty sigh. Darya still had too many questions and doubts floating around in his mind.

"I still don't understand what I am supposed to do. You said move upwards, but how do I get there? I have only ever moved along the ground. No one has ever crawled up the awakening tunnels, and it isn't easy to move around you see. It's the Imperveites, those who follow the new way. They are stopping us, those of us who still look for the sea."

"He is right dear Bahrun. I have journeyed through many tunnels and the situation is the same. The new way is spreading and they are stopping us from carving the walls. I fear them. They no longer act the way Porousees have always acted; they are now becoming more like the humans. What are we supposed to do?"

Bahrun's eyes were still closed, and he seemed to be lost in his own thoughts and dreams, but he answered the question:

"When the one who is close to you is now far away, follow him, though he moves as swiftly as the waves in the sea, and when you feel you can't keep up or you're lost, visualise the waves of the sea, rising and falling beneath your feet. Then they will move you along."

Darya stared blankly. "I don't understand."

"Never fear, my friend, never fear!" laughed Bahrun. "On this journey, you will face two tests and two fears. If you can overcome these frightening things, you will reach your destination."

"What are these fears?" asked Mesi, darkly.

"You will face the fear of harm and the fear of loneliness. When each one assails you, just remember this advice. When harm comes your way, visualise the waves of the sea and they will sweep you away, far away from harm. If you are all alone, without a friend, call on the sea, with love and severe need, and it will pull you along, like a good friend. Just remember this and you will see what there is to see. So onwards and upwards my friends!" Bahrun gazed into the two visitors, wondrously, and then glided away.

"Wait!" cried Darya. "Is there no other way?"

Bahrun turned, the smile widening exquisitely, "Trust your heart my friends, and trust the sea."

And with that, he disappeared around the corner.

Darya and Mesi were still confused as to what they were supposed to do, but they felt safe and free after speaking to Bahrun.

"I can't believe that I met him." sighed Mesi, as they walked out of the cave into the enormous interlinking corridors. "My brothers often sing odes for Bahrun the skipper, and I am the lucky one to have actually met him..." He broke off, his voice breaking from the beautiful tears welling in his face.

"He reminded me of my dreams." remarked Darya, moments later. Fear and woe were still fluctuating in Darya's heart and head. A deep yearning for the past engulfed him. Memories of his old friends and the great times flooded his mind. Then the haunting words of Bahrun rose and fell, "Trust your heart... Trust the sea..." He desperately wanted the certitude that he sensed in Bahrun, but the fear was too much.

"Hey, you two! Stop where you are!"

Bahrun and Mesi stopped in their tracks and looked back with their breaths skipping. Standing in a line, half a tunnel away, stood the same group of Imperveites, led by Callan. They carried rock maces in their hands and seemed to be gripping onto them menacingly.

"You need to come with us!" shouted Callan, marching towards them, followed by his henchmen.

Darya and Mesi were struck with fear. What would they do with those maces?

"I think we had better make a dash for it, Darya."

Darya could not move an inch. Fear of the Imperveites and the clubs they carried gripped onto his legs, fixing him in place. Visions of the humans fighting and beating each other from the tales materialised in his mind. Horror filled him. Terror chilled his eyes. He shuddered at these foreign emotions, but then he heard a voice in his heart:

"Visualise the waves of the sea and they will sweep you away..." Bahrun's advice.

Callan's cruel face and menacing mace were now visible. Instead of swirling Porousee eyes, he had reddened daggers piercing the world around him.

"Darya! Quickly!" Mesi grabbed his hand and tried to pull him away.

Bahrun's words still resonated in Darya's heart. *"Visualise the waves of the sea..."*

Darya closed his eyes, took a deep breath and reached out to the sea with his whole being. Suddenly, a great wind enveloped the pair and, just as Callan and his thugs reached out to grab them, Darya and Mesi felt a tremendous force shift them from below and push them way ahead into the next tunnel, until Callan was merely a dot in the distance.

The spirit left them, they gazed around in awe at their pursuers, almost a whole sleep behind them.

Darya smiled at Mesi. "Visualise the sea..."

***

Darya and Mesi hastened into the next tunnel, took a right into the next cavern then took another right. There were so many interlinking corridors and passages that it was impossible for Callan and his bullies to follow the pair. Eventually, they slowed down and took stock of their surroundings. They stood in another vast tunnel, luminous rock beaming down from above, drenching the area with hazy light. Darya was heartened to see that in this tunnel Porousees still worked away on the patterns, vigorously hammering, etching and shaping the rock face and surfaces.

"Isn't that strange?" remarked Mesi, as he stared at the ceiling and walls around them.

"Yes, it is," replied Darya. For he had noticed, like Mesi, that this tunnel was covered in one, rather stark pattern, in contrast to the rich, variegated matrices of a typical Porousee tunnel. Each Porousee, who hammered above or stood on the side, seemed to be blindly following the same pattern as the carver beside him. Darya and Mesi frowned for they had never seen this type of behaviour before. There was almost an air of sickness about this tunnel. A group of Porousees approached them, holding their patterning tools and grinning but Darya felt repelled for a reason he could not yet understand.

"Ah, some brothers! Some friends!" grinned the first one, wide eyes, wide smile. Darya and Mesi looked at each other, rather uncomfortably. "You are not like those new ones, we can see." he remarked.

The others in the group laughed and smiled in unison, as if they were clones.

"We were just passing through," announced Mesi.

"No, no, not just passing through. You have to stay here where it's safe. You have to stay here and help the cause." The first one spoke with vigour.

"Cause, what cause?" replied Darya.

"Why the fight back, of course. We can not just sit back and allow these misguided friends to destroy our way of living. Have you seen what they are doing? They are kidnapping the new-borns; they are punishing us who want to continue carving; they are holding us against our wills; they are acting like the humans in the stories who used to kidnap other humans and force them to be like them. If they treat us like the humans treat their weak ones, then we must respond as other humans have responded?"

"And what does that mean?" asked Mesi, troubled.

"We must fight back!" he yelled.

And the clones also punched the air and echoed: "We must fight back!"

Their leader continued: "We must use these tools for beautifying our tunnels to fight off the Imperveites! Once they feel a few hard strikes to their foolish heads, they will think twice about interfering with us. Power to the Patterners!"

"Power to the Patterners!" the clones intoned.

And now the group stared at Mesi and Darya.

"We need every bit of help we can get. We have started a new movement, which we believe is the only path to forming the greatest pattern that has ever been formed by our people. We are going to form the one pattern, together, as a collective because we are all one body, one soul, one people. We are not unique, we are part of one rock. This is how the early ones survived in the darkness. We must go back to their ways and forge a new tradition, instead of blindly following the generations before us. We are the inheritors of the early ones!"

"The inheritors of the early ones!" droned the clones.

"I thought the early ones achieved what they did because the beauty of their souls shone from their eyes," interjected Darya.

"Those are just stories, friend," replied the Porousee, unimpressed. "This mystical nonsense is what allowed the disease of the Imperveites to rise. We all realised that these enigmas are just stories passed down without any substance. The substance is in the thinking, in the structure, in the organisation. Our pattern is organised, planned, meticulous and thorough. Our pattern, as you can see, is so exquisite yet methodical; as a collective, we will repel the Imperveites and we will take our way of life forward, into a new direction, which does not necessarily rely on mystical properties like water, oceans or large boats. Our inspiration are those great humans who rose against the tyranny of tradition and decay and revolutionised their societies. We will make our ancestors proud. Power to the Early Ones!"

"Power to the Early Ones!"

"Okay, we get the idea," replied Mesi.

"Yes, we do, but we must be going onwards and upwards. It was great meeting you," said Darya, moving away.

The leader of group motioned to his clones who suddenly stood in front of Darya and Mesi, halting their exit. They turned the other way and headed for the exit in the opposite direction. The clones appeared before them again. Darya and Mesi looked at each other and realised they were facing a real problem. They had unwittingly fallen into a trap.

Anger rose in the lines of Darya's rock veins.

"There is not just one special pattern friend!" declared Darya, with great force. "There are as many patterns as there are rocks in our world. And we, as Porousees, were born to create a unique pattern, every single time we make an imprint onto our walls. There is not one pattern. There are innumerable patterns which all lead onto greatness, just as there are innumerable drops of water which flow into the sea!"

The Porousees listened with growing ire and then erupted.

"Misguidance!"

"Seize him!"

"Blind follower!"

"Ignoramus!"

The group surrounded Darya and Mesi, grabbed them by the arms and legs and then threw them behind a large rock. Inside there was a hollow, like a small cell cut into the rock face. The leader looked down at the two prisoners.

"We do not tolerate those old views anymore. We will give you some time to think about your true purpose in life." Then the leader pushed the rock in front of them, effectively imprisoning them. There was enough room for Darya and Mesi to sit in the hollow, which was mildly lit from the light streaming in from cracks in the great rock.

"We should have brought our tools." said Mesi, despondently.

"Our people are becoming sick. Their hearts and minds are poisoned from these new ideas. What has become of us?" despaired Darya.

"It is as Bahrun said, our world is breaking apart and the sea will take us whether we like it or not." Mesi sighed. "Oh, what I would give just to see one drop of water from the sea..." He closed his eyes and wept. Porousees did not weep the human way, instead they made poignant heaving sounds and sniffed the air like cattle. Mesi cried with an emotion that Darya understood very well: the pain of separation. Separation from the sea. Darya knew this pain because it was what drove him to produce his loving patterns in the walls of their world. He patted Mesi's back sympathetically, while he wept his heart out.

"Just a drop of the sea..." whispered Mesi.

Then, a miracle occurred. Darya stared, his mouth gaping, as he saw a small, round shape appear on Mesi's eye. It was like a tiny bubble and it was slowly rolling down Mesi's face. It left a moist trail as it slid down Mesi's face and Darya suddenly realised what he was witnessing after a memory of one of the human tales surfaced in his mind: the formation of a teardrop. And tears were formed with a similar essence as water... Darya watched the tear roll further down Mesi's still face and became abstracted. Darya could notice a thousand different rock patterns shimmering and manifesting in the teardrop, thrumming like waves in an ocean.

Suddenly, Darya saw a vision of Bahrun before him, like a picture floating in the air, shimmering like a reflection in the water. Bahrun gazed beautifully into Darya's eyes and said:

"*All know that the drop merges into the ocean...*" And the vision faded into the rock.

"Mesi, did you just see that?" asked Darya in wonder.

Mesi did not answer?

"Mesi, my friend, are you okay?"

Still Mesi did not answer. Instead, he abruptly rose to his feet, his eyes looked ahead without expression and he smashed apart the rock obstacle with pounding fists.

"Mesi! What are you doing?"

The Inheritors of the Early Ones all perked up and came running at Mesi. But Mesi advanced at them, unfazed.

"Mesi, wait!" yelled Darya, desperate to get his attention. But Mesi would not listen and strode forward. Then the leader of the Inheritors appeared. He stared at Mesi carefully and then motioned his followers to stop.

"We can do nothing. He is leaving us. He will disappear."

And as Mesi strode away, through the parting Inheritor clones, Darya realised what was happening. His only friend, Mesi, was disappearing, returning to the sea without a shore. His only brother and supporter in this new world of cruel leaders and foolish followers was going and now Darya would be alone. That feeling of loneliness eclipsed the elation that Bahrun's vision gave him. But there was only one thing for it.

"Mesi, my friend, wait!"

The leader watched Darya rush after the disappearing Mesi and motioned his clones to give way:

"There's nothing we can do for these old ones. As the humans says: you can't teach an old dog new tricks. Let him through."

The clones obediently gave way to Darya, who rushed around them and sprinted after Mesi, who moved silently ahead, relentless and quick.

Darya's heart sank as Mesi moved further out of reach. Now he was alone...

***

Darya could not find Mesi anywhere and he had ventured further away from the inhabited tunnels. He stood in a wide, bare tunnel, with precious little light and jagged rocks sticking out at the sides. Up ahead, the way ascended into a vertical shaft. The only way forward was to go upwards. Behind, many tunnels away, the nearest inhabitants were the confounded inheritors. He did not have a choice but to climb up that passage.

Images of Mesi's smile, his hope, his tear and then the vision of Bahrun flashed through his mind. Although Bahrun's words were rather cryptic, Darya understood them in his own way. He had seen how that tear on Mesi's face opened a doorway of some deep, unfathomable meanings. He felt the vastness of the sea in that solitary tear of separation. And now he was the one who felt the sting of separation from his only friend, Mesi, this strange little Porousee from the other tunnels. Without a companion, Darya's heart ached as he was used to company, friendship, brotherhood and cheer. There was no better feeling at the end of a hard day's carving then sitting with the circles of Porousees and listening to the tales and the songs. The animated eyes, the excited voices, the expectant ears, eager to hear the next part of the tale. He stared around at this bland, empty tunnel with no patterns to tell the stories of their race or represent the ocean. Isolation encircled him and then pressed down on his mind.

"My dear sea without a shore! I am nothing but a lonesome lump of rock who is lost in a world he no longer understands. By your infinite presence and innumerable waves, give me some hope, keep me going in the search for you..."

No sooner had Darya made this heartfelt plea that he felt a tremendous lift and an exquisite whispering breeze blew around him and through him, gently guiding him up to the passage. Darya scanned up the shoot and could see depressions where he could easily place his hands and feet. And up he went, guided by the breeze which soothed his heartache and gave him cheer.

It seemed like, in an instant, he had reached the dizzy heights of this vertical shoot. What a miracle! Way below, like a shining dot, he could see the entrance. And above, there was... This is where his breath was taken away. For, a few feet above him, he could see a square-shaped sheet, made of some brown, sinewy material he had never felt before. In the middle of this square was a circular tool, hanging down, its other end lodged in this alien material. He realised what it was: a handle. And he realised what he was facing: the trapdoor... The mythical trapdoor from the stories which opened up to...

It couldn't be, could it? Darya's excitement and awe were overwhelming him, but he fought them off, took a deep breath, reached out to take the handle and gave it a pull. It opened...

All above what quiet; he could not see anything but darkness streaming in from the opening. Perhaps it wasn't what he was hoping for. But he didn't stop there and pulled himself further upwards until he was through the door.

He stood up with his eyes closed, unable to open them. But now he could hear and feel. He felt his whole body swaying ever so slightly side to side. Something was rocking him. And what he could hear was just indescribable. It was a universe of rising and falling whispers, which tantalised every pore in his porous body.

Now he opened his eyes and he gazed in utter wonder. Below him, the passage still stood as it was, but around him was a rickety, tiny vessel, the size of twenty Porousees stuck together. This vessel or raft was floating. Floating in the sea... Yes, all around him, engulfing his view, from every direction, was an endless ocean, with rising and falling waves, shimmering and dazzling. Above, there lay a vast expanse, the sky, and shining warmly, was a perfect round disc: the sun.

Suddenly, the raft gave way, Darya felt himself being enveloped and then he forgot where he was and all he felt was the endless presence of the ocean surging him forward for eternity. This infinite rush washed away his fear, doubts and loneliness and he felt an irrepressible love flow through him endlessly.

The more the sea enveloped him the more he could see. He momentarily found himself on a gargantuan vessel and there he saw every race of human being, black and white-skinned, living, loving, fighting, dying, without realising that their boundaries and horizons were really the borders of the ship and enveloping their ship was the endless sea without a shore. Suddenly, Darya felt himself rising and he noticed how this awe-inspiring sight of a ship and its endless population now appeared like a drop of water which submerged into the sea without a shore. He remembered Bahrun's words: *"All know that the drop merges into the ocean..."* Then, he felt his whole being reduced to a single drop and the whole ship and ocean surged into the drop without spilling out. Then to his delight, he saw Mesi, smiling like the sun shining through clouds, swimming and waving as Darya passed by. His face had the warmest look and most wonderful brightness. Then Darya felt himself disappear and plummet for years and years...

Then, the next moment, Darya found himself in this rickety boat again, climbing down the shoot, pacing back to the tunnels. But with every step that he took, he saw his whole world submerged in the sea without a shore. All his fear and woes were gone and all that he knew was endless lapping of the waves in the sea. He knew that everything was as it should be, despite the convulsions, despite the change. One day, all would have to return to their true origin.

He walked for many sleeps, not encountering any familiar faces, until he emerged into a tunnel where there was a great hullaballoo. He saw two writhing groups of Porousees facing each other like two convulsing armies ready for a showdown. At the front of the first group stood Vaste, and another line of leaders like him, striding forward. Behind them, the Imperveites yelled and shook their fists with great force. On the other side, there stood The Inheritors of the Early Ones, now a formidable throng, with the leader facing his enemies. They yelled and roared, pumping their maces and tools up and down.

One side shouted: "Leave your ignorance or pay the consequences!"

The other side returned: "Leave your misguidance or feel our wrath!"

Dotted around the immense tunnel, staring from behind rocks and boulders were simple Porousees, trying to hide and shield themselves from impending war.

Darya stood tall, unfazed. The sea engulfed every atom of surface and living thing in sight.

Suddenly, Bahrun appeared, seemingly taller and stronger than how he appeared before. He strode forward and yelled at the top of his voice.

"Enough!" It was like a clap of thunder.

The two warring groups settled down and gawked at the lonely Porousee standing away from them.

"I am Bahrun, a drop of water from the sea without a shore." His voice boomed like the stories of Zeus speaking from the clouds. "And I warn you about a day that you can not postpone; a day that the sea will take you back!" The sheer power of his voice had stunned them all.

"So, end your trouble; end your fighting. You must prepare for a journey that you will inevitably take one day."

It was as if the two groups had been muted. Just then, Darya moved forward and caught sight of Bahrun. Bahrun stared into Darya and Darya stared into Bahrun. Silently, they felt the sea rush through them and drown them in its pure waters. They shook hands and embraced like true brothers. Suddenly, all the old Porousees who formed the dance appeared and joined Bahrun and Darya, and then all the hiding Porousees got the strength to emerge from their hiding places. Before long, another vast group formed, eclipsing the two groups who were intent on destruction.

They Imperveites and Inheritors came to their senses, noticed the new third group and sneered. Soundlessly, the two groups dispersed, mumbling bitterly.

Just as he was about to disappear, Vaste turned towards the Porousees and shouted: "You have won the battle today but the war will be ours!" And off he went with his tail between his legs.

Bahrun and Darya took no notice of Vaste. They stood together and then faced their friends.

"My dear friends," began Darya, "Things have changed forever, our friends on the other sides will no longer see us as we did before. But the point is not gaining acceptance or being part of a group. The point is the journey, the journey to sea which awaits us at this very moment. So, there is no time to waste, I will take you to new tunnels which are in dire need of patterns!" The Porousees cheered and shook each other's hands. Bahrun smiled. Suddenly, a teardrop formed on his face and he beamed at Darya. Darya drew closer to Bahrun and whispered: *"But few know the ocean merges into the drop."*

NOTES:

Most know the drop merges into the ocean but few know the ocean merges into the drop.

An aphorism attributed to the mystic Kabir.

Wine
and
Men

"What is she looking at?"

Lucy's friends glanced at her and then at the figure on the other side of the street, who stood watching them, while they sat around the chic table outside a prestigious city wine bar.

"She's been staring at us, or rather at me, for a long time," remarked Lucy, flicking back her gorgeous, auburn hair, taking a long drag of her sleek cigarette nonchalantly, like Greta Garbo.

"I don't think she's looking at you my dear," remarked Lucy's confidante, Roxanne. "She's probably senile."

"A bit creepy though," chimed in their friend Saba. "That's not right the way she's just looking at us."

"Don't stare back!" insisted Lucy. "She might come up to us!"

Roxanne interrupted: "Just ignore her. Pretend she's not even there."

Lucy shuddered slightly; all she could see was a dark dress, a flowing scarf, thick dark hair and intense eyes across the street. But she took heed of her friend's advice and turned back to her conversation.

Roxanne proffered the bottle and then poured the pristine red wine into each of her friends' glasses. Lucy raised a toast.

"Here's to wine and... men!" She grinned and her friends smiled back knowingly.

The three women, elegant, stunning, in their prime, successful in their jobs, well-paid and well-bred, supped on the wine and sighed sweetly as the taste infused them.

"So," began Lucy, "Who are we meeting here tomorrow?"

Roxanne drew closer. "These three guys are cuter than cute! I met them last week at the conference..."

The sun shone, warm and hearty like mulled wine. The central London traffic of taxis, businessmen and politicians ebbed and flowed. The three women stared into each other's vibrant eyes, exalting in the taste of wine, enjoying the thrill of the moment, of being stunning young women who had the world at their feet and all men at their disposal. Their eyes sparkled like stars and all those around them couldn't help but admire these women surreptitiously.

***

"It's her again," whispered Lucy.

It was the heart of the next evening. The three sirens were sitting in the same spot with three charming men, groomed, toned and dashing like film stars. The three companions sat side by side facing their dates, who were chatting away amongst themselves.

"What are you talking about?" enquired Saba.

"It's that woman again."

Roxanne frowned slightly and peered across the street. The woman from the previous day stood there, looking at them.

"Just ignore her, I told you. The more attention you give her, the more she will do it."

"But it's really annoying," complained Lucy.

The guys noticed the hushed tones and looked across the street.

"What's wrong ladies?" began one of them.

"Oh, it's nothing..." Roxanne smiled at Lucy. "So, tell us about your latest project." Roxanne nudged Lucy who was still looking across the road, which impelled her to notice her wine glass, ripe for the taking and the three princes siting opposite her.

"Yes, sorry, it's nothing," Lucy said, gazing playfully at the three men. "Do tell us about your latest exploits."

***

"Why do you keep watching me?"

It was the midday now. Lucy was alone, having a glass of wine with lunch in the glorious sunshine before returning to the office. That irritating woman was once again across the street, seemingly watching her, and Lucy, against her better judgement, left her lunch and wine glass and marched across the street.

She stood there glaring at this singular woman, who Lucy surmised was probably called Babushka, hailed from Romania and was going to ask her for money for her growing brood.

"Well?" demanded Lucy. "What's your problem? Do you even speak English?" The woman seemed to be ignoring her and still looked across the road, but turned and Lucy was taken aback.

There they were: those clear, dark eyes, thick, healthy locks underneath a loosely-draped headscarf. She was strange and beautiful like a flower in a rainforest, like a newly discovered sea creature, but what business did this woman have with her?

"I'm sorry to disturb you," replied the woman. Her accent had a trace of eastern places, but she spoke perfect estuary English. Her voice was soft like silk and high like a flute. There was a hint of melancholy about her; something tragic. Perhaps she was a refugee, thought Lucy.

"But as I have walked by here, I have seen you, and I couldn't help noticing something."

Half-interested in the impending response, Lucy asked: "And what was that?"

The woman drew closer and whispered:

"I think you have a thing for wine and men."

Suddenly, Lucy erupted in laughter, which also infected the stranger, and for a moment, the two giggled away like a pair of long-lost friends. Then Lucy returned to her senses, wiping her eyes.

"What on earth are you talking about? Do I know you?" After the initial hilarity of this stranger's outlandish comment, now Lucy was becoming deeply irritated because it seemed that this woman had not only been eavesdropping on her conversations, but was also making some sort of moral judgement.

"I was just making an observation, that's all." remarked the woman, smiling.

A scowl was beginning to form on Lucy's face.

"Well, thank you, but please keep your observations to yourself. Please stop staring at us across the road. It's rude and I will call the police and have you done for harassment if you do it again."

The strange woman seemed not to register Lucy's offence and threat and carried on unperturbed.

"Well, I also love wine, a very special sort of wine. And I know someone... Just the mention of his name makes me swoon and every time I see him, it's like the whole universe and all it contains vanishes and there is only his beauty and his love."

Lucy was dumbstruck momentarily. She couldn't really believe what she was hearing.

"Pardon me?" she asked in disbelief.

"I said, I know him. He is more beautiful than any man your eyes have ever looked upon and the wine he gives you tastes so sweet, it will make your heart melt. I can take you to him. See him for yourself, take the cup and taste his wine. Don't you love wine and men?"

The woman gazed at Lucy firmly, meaningfully. Lucy, still in a stupor, thought for a moment and then couldn't help herself. Fits of laughter shivered through her as she registered what the woman had said and what she had expected her to say. It felt like she had just entered the twilight zone! What Lucy had expected was that this woman would eventually lead her onto a story about a daughter who was suffering from a life-threatening illness and she needed money or her daughter would die. What she got instead was something like a genie's promise in Arabian Nights!

"So?" asked the woman, brightly. "Would you like to join me for some of this fine wine?"

Sensible thought returned to Lucy like the kick you get from a stiff coffee on a morning after a night out.

"No, I think I'll leave it this time." *Either she is a rather unhinged individual or she could take me around the corner where a van full of women traffickers lay in wait*, thought Lucy.

The woman's transparent eyes gazed into Lucy's. She smiled widely.

"You have nothing to fear. The place where you can taste this wine and see my friend is just a few minutes' walk from here and you know this is a very busy road with plenty of people. There is even CCTV all over this street. I am no criminal. I just believe we share common interests and I thought I would share something with you because you might appreciate it. But if you are unconvinced, never mind. I will not bother you again."

There was something convincing, reasonable and even harmless in her words and ways. It couldn't do any harm to follow this woman up the road. And if it meant she would finally leave her and her friends alone, perhaps it was a good move, thought Lucy.

"Okay, then, lead the way!"

So, they started walking up the bustling street, full of various people disappearing and reappearing out of the plethora of cafes and wine bars that populated this fashionable area of the city. The woman walked ahead of Lucy and intermittently peered back, smiling graciously.

She wore a fine olive coloured long dress, like a tunic, which flowed around her body beautifully. The scarf hung gracefully around her head, with lustrous wavy locks hanging out, which she would flick back behind the scarf. Her face was wide and full like the sky and her eyes were so clear it seemed as if they had been purified like the unblemished water of mountain streams and pools.

After a few minutes, they were on the opposite end of the road, which was the high street for a variety of ethnicities. Restaurant, kebab shops and grocers filled this side of the street. Now the woman came to a halt outside a building and pointed.

"This is the place."

Lucy read the sign above the door. Embassy mosque. There were two doors, one which said: "Brothers' entrance" and the other which said: "Sisters' entrance".

"I don't understand." Lucy began.

"This is the place. Where you can see him, where he gives you his wine."

"In a mosque?" asked Lucy incredulously.

The woman beamed at her in response.

Sighing deeply, Lucy fumed: "Well, you have truly wasted my time. No offence, but I think we'll end the conversation here. I will leave you to your wine and your man. Now can you leave me and my friends alone from now on?"

The woman gazed back at Lucy, sympathetically.

"Okay, it is your choice, but let me leave you with this..." She began to recite verses that Lucy had never heard before, heartfelt, deep as the ocean, as passionate as Dionysian lovers. Then she disappeared into the sisters' door of the Embassy mosque. Lucy walked back to the wine bar, sat at her table quietly and sipped on her wine then returned to work.

***

The next day, Lucy met Roxanne and Saba for lunch at the wine bar. They were nattering away about work and the fact that Roxanne was seeing one of the guys they met the other night, when suddenly there was shrieking and commotion across the street.

"Oh dear Lucy, looks like your friend is in trouble!" laughed Roxanne. The three watched as a ragged old woman across the street was fighting off two female police officers who were trying to lead her away.

Lucy was confused: "What do you mean by 'your friend'?"

"You know, your friend. That woman who's been watching us every time we sit here."

Lucy looked again at the screaming old woman, who was grappling the officers: "That's not her."

"Yes it is! That's the one we saw before, when the guys were with us and that other time as well."

"Roxanne, that is definitely not her," stated Lucy, rather passionately.

"Lucy dear. I am quite sure that is the strange old woman that you complained about before. I saw her too," confirmed Saba.

Lucy looked back at the bedraggled drunken woman with her haggard looks who was now being dragged along by the police into the waiting police car. That was not the woman she had spoken to and walked with. But Lucy did not want to betray her thoughts to her friends.

"Oh, perhaps it was her then. I could have sworn she looked different before though."

"These poor alcoholics are like Jekyll and Hyde. I guessed she had it coming. Somebody must have complained to the police."

Lucy felt deeply disquieted as she reflected on what had just occurred. Roxanne and Saba had seen an alcoholic old woman. She had seen this mysterious eastern woman who had led her to the mosque down the road. Had she hallucinated it all? Was she ill? Or perhaps the woman she had spoken to was somebody else? But she can't have been because she had referred to what had transpired before. What on earth was going on?

So, later, after work, Lucy approached the Embassy mosque rather gingerly. The identity of this stranger had been bugging her all day. She had to find out who this woman was to confirm her own sanity. She opened the door of the sisters' entrance and found herself in a hallway, which at the end was signed: prayer hall. Doors to the side had signs that said: Ablutions and Toilets.

There was a Muslim woman standing in the corridor, with a headscarf and long dress reading a noticeboard. What on earth was Lucy going to do? How could she bring up the subject? Do you know any strange women talking about wine and men in this mosque? Oh no! That would certainly be taken in the wrong way. Nevertheless, she walked up to the noticeboard and stood alongside the woman who was reading the notice on children's classes. Lucy scanned her side of the noticeboard.

It was here that her heart skipped a beat and butterflies wreaked havoc below.

There, on the noticeboard, was a photo of the woman she had spoken to. The clear eyes, the rich hair, the melancholic smile. Underneath was written:

From Allah did we come and to Him we will return.
Quran reading for Layla Habeeb this Saturday. All sisters are invited.

Lucy stared closely at the photograph. It was unmistakably the same woman who had spoken of wine and men. Layla Habeeb was her name. And the women were reading Quran for her. What did this mean?

"Excuse me but can you tell me who that is?" asked Lucy politely to the woman beside her.

"Oh, that's Layla. She was one of our sisters..."

"Was?" interrupted Lucy, her heart beginning to palpitate.

"Yes, she passed away last week. She was like a spiritual woman. People used to come to her for prayers and help. She was beautiful."

"Oh, I see, thank you."

"Why do you ask? Did you know her?"

"Er, no, not really. I only spoke to her once..." Bewilderment was beginning to flood Lucy's mind. This Layla had died last week, but she had spoken to her and walked with her yesterday.

"Where did you meet her?"

"Oh, I met her once on the street outside. It's sad she passed away."

"Yes, very sad," replied the woman.

"Where was she buried?" asked Lucy, her voice quivering from her inner turmoil.

"She was buried in the cemetery up the road. You know, the local one. You can pay your respects there if you want to. She's in the Muslim section at the back."

"Okay, thank you, I may go there soon."

"Nice to meet you. What's your name?"

"I'm Lucy."

"I'm Aisha. And by the way, if you want somewhere to sit and reflect, you are welcome to come and sit here in peace."

"That's very kind of you to offer, thank you," replied Lucy and she was just about to go when the question that had been aching in her head tumbled out.

"When I spoke to her, she talked of wine and men. Was she okay? I didn't think Muslims were into that sort of thing."

The woman laughed: "Oh no! She didn't mean that sort of wine or those sort of men...Yes, she did speak like that. As I said, she was spiritual and sometimes she did utter some mystifying things. Go to her grave and see it. You'll like it."

Lucy veered out of the mosque and found herself involuntarily striding up the street towards the local cemetery. Her mind and soul were wrestling furiously. Had she really spoken to Layla? Was she going crazy? How could she talk to someone who died the week before? What was happening to her?

It was only when she reached the graveyard and stood before Layla Habeeb's grave that her spirit floored her rationality and a mixture of horror, confoundment, and strange ecstasy shivered through her body. For on Layla's tombstone were inscribed the very same verses that Layla had recited to her the day before. Lucy read them as the tears poured down her face:

When my lonely heart befriended the wine-giver
Wine fired my heart and my veins filled up
But when His image all my eyes possessed
A voice descended
"Well done, O sovereign Wine and Peerless Cup!"

Notes:

The final verses were taken from: "The Wine of Love" by Jalalul Din Rumi, from *Rumi Poet and Mystic*, translated by Reynold A Nicholson.

Beyond

The

Storm

I was roaming outside on the vast fields under the tearful sky searching for my beloved one.

I lost her the previous night, while I slept, while I drifted through the valleys of discontentment in my dreams. When I awoke, she was gone... And realising my folly, I rushed out of my house searching desperately for her. Searching up trees, walking into caves, scaling the solitary hills of woe. I had not found her and I was becoming a nervous wreck of a soul.

Before I left, I rang my teacher and asked him what I should do. He asked:

"Who do you love the most?"

I replied: "She who possesses my innermost soul. When I am quiet, she is in my thoughts, when I am speaking, she is all that I speak of. And now I have lost her." I began to sob. "I lost her when I slipped into the valleys of my fears and walked down those descending plains into oblivion."

My teacher stopped me with a firm voice, saying: "Well, get out there and find her! Search for her everywhere. Retrieve your beloved. Find her once again and do not be afraid of the outside. Keep going through the storms that will come, keep going through the hills, although you find nothing is there. But watch out for a wretched one... He will be out on the fields, sowing seeds of discontentment. Do not listen to what he says and embrace the storm."

So I left. Oscillating between hope and fear, love for her and deep self-loathing. How could I have lost her?

I walked on and on, through the fields of despair, climbed through forests of guilt and scaled great hills of loneliness. Wherever I roamed, I was all alone. There was no sign of her. When would I find her? Where could she be?

Suddenly, thunder clapped, as savagely as two mountain gods crashing against each other. The wind howled like an angry ghost and remorseless clouds, dark and thick as the earth, crowded the sky. I happened to be traversing an expanse of farm land, interrupted by rows of ominous trees, when I came across a crooked old man, with sharp eyes and sharp nails. He stood there, holding large seeds, which wriggled and hissed like snakes, in his prickly fingers. He was planting them in the ground. His cutting eyes looked upon me as I walked by.

He said: "Go home my friend. A storm is about to come. You can not outlast it. All your efforts are in vain. You will not find her and this storm will consume you and spit you out into the sea. Retreat to the safety of your home. Find someone else to love. There are plenty of beauties in your street. Look to them instead."

His words became wretched, poisonous worms that crawled into my ears and began burrowing away inside.

Thunder grumbled and roared throughout the sky; the wind pushed me backwards like a big bully. Those thoughts crawled deep inside and the old man wore a wide smile.

"You'll never find her; you'll never find her. You can not survive the storm. Retreat! Retreat! Go back to your cosy bed. Go back to your dreams of despair. The wind is too strong; the thunder will deafen you; the lightning will burn you up!"

I stopped in my tracks and began looking behind me. Could it be true? Perhaps I had lost her for good? Perhaps she did not want to be found by me. Perhaps she had found someone else... Then I remembered the words of my teacher.

"Watch out for a wretched one... Sowing seeds of discontentment."

"No!" I yelled at the old man, who gawked at me in astonishment. "I will embrace the storm!"

Suddenly, rain poured on me like someone had opened a cosmic tap in the sky; the wind increased in its intensity, battering me, blasting me and I struggled to move ahead.

I could not see that old man any longer, but the worms still crawled deep inside.

"You can not find her; you can not find her; you can not beat the storm..."

This is when I sobbed and called out: "My darling! My only love! I can not go on without you! Help me to find you! A storm has come; worms have entered my heart and I am afraid!"

The rain continued to blast me; the thunder deafened me and the wind bruised me. But still I pushed forward, beyond my fears and beyond my hopes.

When, as if by miracle, when all hope was fading away into the horizon, I stepped out of the storm and found that the air was sweet; the sky was clear and the sun shone kindly.

Beside me stood a willow tree, with branches and leaves hanging down, like the lustrous locks of a goddess. And there behind the tree, beyond the sun and the sky, beyond the earth, so near and so far, I found her, gazing straight into my heart. The worms disappeared; my woes swept away; I sighed as the sweetness shivered within. I had found her. I had found her beyond the storm.

Abdul Razzaq and Abdul Ghani

There once were two men: Abdul Razzaq and Abdul Ghani.

Abdul Razzaq was a faithful man, who was very resourceful, with a talent for acquiring wealth. By the age of forty, he had paid off the mortgages of three properties, rented them out and his portfolio continued to grow promisingly.

He spent on local projects and was always generous to the masjid and community. When his daughters got married, he gave them each lavish send offs, inviting the whole community and ensuring everyone left the hall with a satisfied smile on their faces. His wife was always cheerful and regularly invited the local ladies around her luxuriant house to read Quran and send blessings on the Prophet, Allah bless him and grant him peace. This house was always blessed with the pitter-patter of his daughters' children, with guests from Pakistan, with local dignitaries and businessmen.

The only thing they seemed to lack was sons. But both husband and wife were grateful for what Allah had given them and inwardly they were content. When the couple passed on, it was noticed that a hint of a smile appeared on their faces and people reported that they had heard the shahadah from their lips. Thereafter, Abdul Ghani was lauded and remembered as an exceptional individual, who had lived the best life possible, rich in this world and rich in the next world.

Abdul Ghani was a contemporary of Abdul Razzaq, who lived some two miles away from Razzaq's spacious, detached property on the outskirts of town. Indeed, the two men were frequently seen standing next to each other in the congregational prayers at the mosque. But unlike Razzaq, Abdul Ghani had struggled to make ends meet throughout his life, with jobs in factories, two of which had laid him off, and taxi jobs. He had never been clever enough to multiply his wealth and, for decades and decades, he had to graft just to make ends meet.

His worldly possessions did not amount to much: a terraced house in a cramped area of town and an old people carrier which doubled up as a taxi. His only child and son, Hasan, inherited his dad's artlessness and did not amount to much at school, ending up working in the local supermarket. Hasan was wedded off in Abdul Ghani's ancestral village in Kashmir and it took Hasan and his father several years of hard work to call the bride to England. Mrs Ghani was a simple woman who seldom complained and phlegmatically moved to each phase of her life, enshrouded in her white chadour and her few friends, whom she would call to her house from time to time.

And that's how Ghani lived, until old age took him and his wife. Fate had it that the next available space in the local graveyard was next to Abdul Razzaq. So, there the two graves stood: Abdul Razzaq's marble gravestone, inscribed with exquisite calligraphy and Abdul Ghani's cheap and cheerful piece with the plain inscription from the Quran: From Allah did we come and to Him we will return.

One day, after a burial nearby, two old acquaintances of Razzaq stood before these two graves.

"Our friend, Abdul Razzaq. What a man! So generous, such a good Muslim. Masha Allah, he had been blessed with such wealth and I will never forget that smile on his face when he passed on."

The other looked at Abdul Ghani's grave: "Abdul Ghani... Poor man, he worked so hard..."

That night, these two men saw some familiar faces in their dreams. The first man saw Abdul Razzaq with a face radiant and pure, but there seemed to be a weight on his back.

"How is it with you Abdul Razzaq?"

"Life is blessed." replied Abdul Razzaq. "This world is better than yours, but all the wealth that I did not use for His pleasure has become a burden on my back."

The other man saw Abdul Ghani, enlightened, princely, ennobled.

"How is it with you Abdul Ghani?"

"In the dunya, I was nobody. No one thought of me much or praised my name. But every penny I had, I spent for His sake, and when everyone was asleep, I used to wake up and praise His name. Now the angels visit me in a lush garden filled with exquisite fruit. His sincere remembrance has the highest value here, and money... Money means nothing here, except what was for Allah..."

ABOUT THE AUTHOR

Novid Shaid is an English teacher from the UK, who has taught English in various secondary schools for over fifteen years. He shares short stories and poems on his website, www.novid.co.uk, and has published a novel, The Hidden Ones. His published works are available on Amazon.